ITS NEVER TOO LATE

STORMI MAXWELL

1

The clear blue ocean water steadily crashed into the lifeless machine, leading it to rock in a taunting rhythm. The sun was scorching and reflecting off the waves, causing sweat to build on the nape of her neck. Fury built inside her stomach as she opened the front compartment and searched for anything that could assist in getting the craft started again. Pulling out a flare gun, she swelled with hope. As she opened the device, her heart sank. A flare gun with no flares, if only she could use her explosive anger as a signal.

Renee Martin is a powerfully successful lawyer back home, but out here in the vast open water, she is as helpless as a kitten up a tree. Her phone was useless, being there was no service. She didn't expect any and only brought it to take a picture of proof for her coworkers.

Renee took this time to curse them out individually in her mind. The trip to Galveston Island was their gift to her. After throwing her a surprise divorce party, they told her it was time to get away and reset herself. Renee tried to refuse, arguing there was too much work to leave behind. Her protests fell on deaf ears, as the group insisted that she should spoil herself after the ugly mediation with her ex.

The stipulation was to try something new each day of her trip and post it to her social media. Renee felt naive. She was too old to brag online. Forty-three and stubborn, she had little interest in stepping out of her comfort zone. She had reluctantly turned off the craft to snap her first selfie, and the damn jet ski refused to start again.

Renee regretted choosing the first boat tour and rental place she saw without researching the reviews online. Checking into the hotel, she saw the large sign across the street and figured it would be a great way to start her solo adventure. *Island Connections* seemed like a fitting name for the theme of her vacation, and this was something she would have never done alone.

Now feeling like a foolish castaway, Renee wondered how she would escape this predicament. She had traveled farther than she had intended, the rip tide pulling her farther out still. Renee forced herself to stay calm, stifling the panic building inside her.

Searching deep in the compartment, she found nothing of use. There was a mini fire extinguisher, a whistle, an orange flag, and a flashlight. She stared at the flashlight, praying she would not have to use it.

Leaning into the front of the jetski, her long black hair draped over her face. Renee was unaware of the fishing boat approaching her. The horn blared behind her, causing her to jolt and almost flip over the machine. Turning around, a sense of relief washed over her, and she began to wave her arms manically at the oncoming vessel.

As it got closer, Renee noticed a young man standing shirtless on the bow. He had cut the engine and let the small ship float closer. Looking like a young Posiden, his chest and arms were tan and chiseled with muscles. He held an enormous fishing rod in his hand instead of a trident. His hair was shoulder-length and bleached from the sun. There were tattoos painted on his arms, creeping up and over his broad shoulders.

Renee stood dumbfounded, still floating defenseless in the water.

"Looks like you could use some help," he shouted to her from above.

His deep voice boomed over the sound of the susurration. Ordinarily, Renee would have no trouble answering, but the presence of the young stranger had her completely tongue-tied.

"Are you alright?" he asked, concerned at her silence.

Embarrassed, Renee snapped herself back to reality. "I am fine, but this machine refuses to start."

"If you come aboard, I can take a look for you," he said kindly.

Renee studied his face. The dangers of trusting an unfamiliar man alone on the ocean lingered in the back of her mind, but she felt that she had no other option.

"My name is Jonathan," he said, putting down the rod and reaching for her hands.

"Thank you, Jonathan," she started. His strength lifted her up and over the rail of the boat, catching her off guard.

"Renee," she said breathlessly, "My name is Renee."

Jonathan helped her catch her footing on the deck. "How long have you been floating out here?"

He was still holding her hands.

"I think about fifteen minutes," she said.

The sun glistened off his body, making his skin appear as if it was sparkling. Renee realized she was staring when he smiled at her playfully. She quickly escaped his grasp and nervously folded her arms across her life jacket.

"Let me take a look," he said, "don't go stealing my boat now, okay?"

Renee laughed anxiously. Now was not her first time seeing an attractive man in a bathing suit. She could not believe how his presence had affected her ability to converse. Something about Jonathan had her fumbling like a schoolgirl.

Uncomfortable, she watched as he pulled the strings on his swim trunks, tying them tighter. They were pure white, clean, and crisp like the clouds in the sky. His dark tan skin seemed like polished bronze against the contrast of the fabric.

Jonathan approached the rail and dove into the water, looking like an athletic competitor. The small splash interrupted the oncoming waves, then no evidence of the intrusion remained.

Jonathan surfaced a minute later, shaking his wet hair back and away from his face. He swam closer to the dead craft with powerful strokes and placed his hands on the back.

Renee wanted to look away, but as he lifted his body out of the water with his large forearms, her mouth hung open, and he emerged from the ocean, somehow more gorgeous than when he dove in. His back muscles danced with every movement while he inspected the jet ski.

"Battery is dead," he called up, "I do not have a charger on board. I will have to tow you back."

Glancing up at Renee, he smiled, waiting for her to reply. She quickly snapped her mouth closed and nodded in agreement.

"Unless you would like to take your chances with another passing ship?" he laughed.

"No, that would be great," she said, "I am sorry. The heat is making me lightheaded."

Jonathan's expression changed to concern. "You should sit down and get comfortable. We will be back to shore soon. There is water in the cooler by the cabin door."

Renee did as he instructed. She found the cold water bottles and sat near the front of the boat. Renee watched Jonathan as he used a rope to tow the machine behind them. She wondered why she had to lie to him about being dizzy. She forced herself to regain her witts.

"There, that should do it," Jonathan boarded the boat from the rear ladder and approached her.

"Thank you so much for your help," she said.

Jonathan ran his fingers through his wet honey hair. His white shorts were now saturated and clinging tightly to his lower half. Renee could feel herself blush.

"You aren't from around here," he said.

"Is it that obvious," Renee chuckled and looked out towards the horizon.

"I didn't mean anything by that," he said softly, "I should have asked you where you are from."

Jonathan walked over to the cooler, grabbed a water bottle, and sat beside her. His shorts made a wet sloshing sound against the vinyl seat.

"No, I am from Texas, just not this part of Texas," she laughed.

"Ah," he said smiling, "let me guess, "Houston?"

"Austin."

"That was my second guess," Jonathan said and scooted closer to her.

Renee stiffened at his movement. His legs were almost touching her bare thigh, making her breath quicken.

"Can you swim, Renee?" he asked. His voice was low. Renee felt her heartbeat in her ears.

"Yes," she replied, staring at his lips.

"Are you a strong swimmer?" Jonathan grinned.

Renee raised an eyebrow at the question, wondering what relevance that had.

"Yes?" she answered.

Jonathan lifted his hands to the buckles on her life vest and opened one. "Then you don't have to sit uncomfortably in this thing the whole way back."

She held her breath as he popped the remaining clasps too quickly for her to protest, exposing her body to the hot sun. Renee was wearing an aquamarine bikini, another decision she would have never made. With the help of her vacation planners, she bought it to break her lackluster wardrobe.

Jonathan was watching her as she pulled the vest away from her frame. Renee may be forty-three, but she was in great shape. She was disciplined with exercise and eating healthily. She pulled off the swimsuit rather well.

His eyes wandered over her body and met her pale blue eyes. "That is a beautiful color on you."

Renee was surprised by the sudden compliment and shifted nervously on the seat.

"I can't believe the battery died," she said, desperate to change the subject.

"It happens," he shrugged.

Leaning back, he took a long drink of water.

"Yeah, well, when I looked inside the front compartment. There was nothing useful, just a flareless flare gun," she said, annoyed.

Jonathan sat quietly, turning his gaze to the water.

"I guess I should have read more reviews about the place before I jumped on the first ski I could find," she said, "Who runs a business like that?"

Jonathan pressed his lips together and stood. "I suppose we should be getting you back."

Renee looked up at him. His lack of conversation had her wondering if he was listening to her.

Jonathan started walking to the helm.

Renee leaned back in the seat and pulled her hair away from her face. She relaxed as Jonathan started the boat and made his way back to shore. She sighed deeply. Today's adventure had her rattled, but she was grateful to sneak a few glances at the strong man steering the ship.

He was too young for her, but for a moment, she thought he was flirting. Renee shook off the feeling and blamed the heat for her erratic thoughts.

It did not take long to reach the shoreline, and Jonathan navigated the boat through the various channel buoys. Renee stood to tell him the rental company, but to her surprise, he pulled right up to *Island Connections* dock.

She picked up her life preserver and walked toward the side of the boat. Before she could ask him how he knew where to go, the young man who processed her payment earlier ran out to catch the line and secure them to the ties.

"Hey, boss," he shouted to Jonathan and ran around the front to grab the next tie.

"We have a dead battery, Chris," Jonathan called back to him.

Renee stood, confused at the exchange.

"Miss Martin," Chris looked shocked.

She smiled uncomfortably at the young man and brought the vest up to shield her body. Renee shot a look back to Jonathan, mortified by her earlier insult.

Jonathan had hopped off the boat and stood on the dock, waiting to assist her. He held out his hand as she approached him.

"You own this rental company?"

"Rentals and tours," he corrected her.

"I am so sorry," she said and felt her cheeks flush again.

"Don't be ridiculous," he said, "I am the one who is sorry. You were right. The flare gun thing was a bad look."

"I didn't know-"

"Of course, you didn't," he said as she stepped off the vessel. Her knees wobbled on the sturdy ground. Jonathan held her hand and pulled her closer to him. Renee was stunned by his boldness.

"Let me make it up to you," he said. He ran his thumb over Renee's knuckles.

"It's okay," she said.

"There is a boat tour tomorrow morning at ten. Please join me. I can prove my business is worth more than the two-star review," he said.

"Two stars is generous," she laughed back playfully.

A devilish grin crossed his lips. "Tomorrow at ten. It was nice to meet you, Renee."

He turned and walked around the back of the building.

Renee stood in wonderment. The exchange left her giddy. Chris approached, handing her the bag of belongings from the jet ski in exchange for the life preserver.

"I apologize for the inconvenience this afternoon Miss Martin," he said, "we were lucky Jonathan was out fishing today and could help."

"Yes, very lucky," she said, smiling.

2

─────────

Renee had trouble falling asleep. When she did finally drift off, her dreams were invaded by Jonathan's tan body, floating atop beautiful turquoise waves. The tribal tattoos on his arms moved like tentacles on his skin. Renee woke multiple times, sweating from the heat of her subconscious, and finally cranked up the air conditioning and rested across the sheets.

Her skin was warm from a light sunburn. The cool sheets helped soothe the uncomfortable sting. When the alarm buzzed, Renee was unsure if she was still dreaming. The hours escaped the night quickly, and she was left feeling anxious.

Considering the point was to relax on vacation, she did not feel she was doing an adequate job. She rolled over and turned off the intrusive sound. Renee stared at the ceiling, wondering if she should go across the street for the boat tour or go back to sleep. Her phone dinged with an alert. Leaning back to the nightstand, she looked at the screen.

It was a text from her receptionist Sarah.

We hope you are having a great time! Here is your daily reminder to get out there and try something new!

Renee frowned at the message. The timing was more than coincidental.

She got up to start another seaside adventure.

The coffee from the hotel lobby burnt the tip of her tongue. She brought the cup down fast, spilling tiny drops on the white sundress.

"Damn it," Renee cursed loud enough for an older couple at the front desk to turn around. She lifted her hand apologetically. The effort to blot the coffee out of the fabric with a beverage napkin had little success. The strangers gave her a look of disapproval for her word choice this early in the day.

Renee tossed the coffee and napkin in the trash and inhaled deeply, walking quickly out of the front door to the crosswalk. She had her bag slung across her shoulder full of her essentials. It tapped lightly against her hip with each hurried step.

Approaching Jonathan's building, Renee's nerves were in her throat. It was unusual for her to feel this way about anyone. She chalked it up to being alone on this beautiful island. All the tourists walking around seemed to be couples of all ages. Renee had noticed few single women.

The sign on the door said closed, and she rolled her eyes. Checking her watch, it was nine forty-five. She was early, but wondering if this was a sign.

She turned to retreat to the hotel when a bell rang behind her. It was Chris. He smiled politely at her.

"Jonathan is around back," he said.

"Thanks," she smiled as he closed the door.

Renee moved around the building and toward the docks. The ocean water was a clear blue-green and hit the wooden piers lightly as her sandals taped along the planks.

She allowed the wind to blow back her long black hair. She closed her eyes and inhaled the sea air. It smelled like clean salt, waking up her senses.

Her moment of serenity was interrupted by vulgarity from a voice behind her.

"Shit!" Jonathan shouted, throwing a metal wrench into a toolbox. The crash caused her to jump and turn around.

As Renee approached, she noticed his arms covered in silky black oil. Renee watched him as he continued to work on the motor. He was wearing a navy blue shirt splattered with stains.

"Looks like you need saving this time," she said to him coyly.

Jonathan jumped at the sound of her voice. Looking up, he greeted her with a wide grin.

"I wasn't sure if you would show," he said.

"I was not either," she laughed nervously.

"Well, I am glad you did," Jonathan placed his tools down and climbed out of the mess. "I apologize for my appearance."

"Do not apologize-" Renne started but was cut short.

Jonathan lifted the t-shirt over his broad shoulders, exposing his chest again. Renee wanted to look away, but her eyes seemed glued to the sight of his bronze skin. She fumbled with her bag and pulled out her dark sunglasses. Placing them on her face to camouflage her stare.

Jonathan wiped off his hands with his dirty shirt, then tossed it aside on top of the abandoned tools. He stepped closer to her and scratched his neck.

Renee was startled by how close he was but remained rooted to the dock.

"Let me just grab a shirt, then we can head out," he said to her softly.

Renee watched him disappear inside the office and waited for the other tourists to arrive for the excursion. She was excited to see the island from the water, not having to worry about being stranded at sea.

She took the opportunity to pull up her long dark hair, exposing her sculpted shoulders and collarbone, hoping to work on her tan in the hot tropical sun.

Jonathan emerged from the door sporting a fresh white shirt and gray shorts, shouting back at Chris.

"I am taking Miss Martin out for the afternoon. No tours today, just rentals," he said.

Renee's expression was unclear under her dark glasses, but her stomach was knotted with dread.

"Not the dead battery ski," he winked at Renee.

"No one else will be joining us?" she asked, uneasy.

Jonathan jumped aboard a much larger boat and reached out his hand. Renee hesitated and pursed her lips tightly together.

His wicked smile was captivating. There was no need to press further. He wiggled his fingers, motioning to come closer. Renee puffed out deeply and accepted his help onto the large ship.

Chris was there to untie the ropes and wave them off as Jonathan took the helm. He started the engine with ease. Renee set down her bag and walked to the rail, admiring the view and ignoring her gut.

"Renee," he called to her, "come closer so you can get the narrated experience."

She turned and approached him slowly, her white dress dancing in the breeze. She could not help but smile at the strong captain smirking back at her.

"Okay," she said, "where do I stand for optimal touring?"

She stopped a few feet away, and Jonathan frowned. Letting go of the wheel, he walked over to her and grabbed her hand. His palm was warm on her skin, and Renee could feel goosebumps form up her arm. He pulled her to the helm and placed her hands on the large metal wheel.

"This is a terrible idea," she said, scared.

"You asked for the best view," hc chuckled.

"I do not want to crash this thing," she said nervously, scanning the water for other ships and floating buoys.

Jonathan stretched his arms lazily over his head and teased her. "I could use a day off."

"Jonathan, please," she begged, "I am not a boater."

He stepped behind Renee, bringing each arm around her body and grabbing the wheel next to her hands. She started to retract, but he pressed his back into her, forcing her to remain standing close to the helm.

"Put your hands back on the wheel, Renee," he said in her ear. His breath was warm on her skin, making her body melt like butter.

Her mind raced. This was different from what she had expected for their tour. Lifting her arms, she did as he asked.

Jonathan placed his large hands over hers and squeezed them lightly. He guided the ship between the floating obstacles, all while explaining the sailor's jargon.

Renee was barely paying attention to the lesson. The sensation of his body distracted her from concentrating. He smelled like the sea. His body was as inviting as the sun's rays.

"Notice how the water is brown closer to the shore there?" he said, pointing to the left. "That is because of sediment turnover. People think our water is murky or dirty, but it is the silt in the water."

Renee nodded and tried to relax her body.

"When there are a lot of swells from the gulf, it creates that brown water," he explained, "it is not always that color."

The ship cleared the last channel marker and was finally out in the open water. Jonathan released his grasp, and Renee took the opportunity to escape from the proximity.

Jonathan let the craft travel farther into the open blue water, colliding with the oncoming waves. Renee listened as he presented more information about the area. His arms moved as he spoke.

"You are very knowledgeable," she said when he paused to idle the ship.

"Thanks," he said, "I better be, considering I am doing this for a living."

Renee chuckled and crossed her arms. "Did you grow up here?"

Jonathan nodded his head. "My pops left me the touring business when he passed away a few years ago. I added the rentals knowing that tours are not as popular as they once were."

Her phone chimed from her bag. Renee walked over to retrieve it.

Sarah had messaged her demanding the obligatory adventure photo.

Renee cursed quietly, contemplating throwing the phone into the waves below.

"Everything alright?" Jonathan asked her, sensing her frustration.

"Yes, it is just my coworker," she said, turning on the camera and lifting her arm to take a picture of the view.

"You are on vacation," Jonathan laughed, "tell them work can wait."

"It is not that," Renee explained, "I was given this trip under the premise I step out of my comfort zone and provide photo evidence of my adventures."

"Shit sounds like you work with a couple of prosecutors," he laughed.

"Actually," she looked up from the camera and furrowed her brow.

"You are a lawyer?" he said in disbelief.

"What? I do not look like a lawyer to you?" she asked, slightly annoyed.

"No, I guess you don't," he said, lowering his voice and stepping closer. "I've never met a lawyer who radiates beauty like you."

Jonathan grabbed the phone from her hand and stepped back, snapping a picture of her against the ocean backdrop. He then reached out to the cell and playfully pulled it away before she could grab it.

He raised his arm high and took a selfie with her smirking behind him.

"There, that should appease the masses," he said, returning the device.

Renee noticed he had sent the two photos to Sarah. The replies would be coming in quickly at the sight of her seaside companion. Deciding to turn the phone off, she tucked it back in her bag and faced Jonathan.

Jonathan turned the boat back toward the docks and began explaining the coastline and different businesses and adventures located around the island. Renee watched him in his element. The way he commanded the large vessel so naturally put her at ease. He continued, and her mind wandered to his subtle compliments and touches. Renee tried desperately to brush them off, but she yearned for more. Jonathan was making her feel young again, something she had given up on after the divorce.

Jonathan brought the boat up effortlessly as they got closer to the dock. Chris ran out like clockwork, securing them to the anchors.

Turning to Renee, his expression turned serious.

"I hope the tour was better than two stars," he said.

She smiled. "Yes, it was at least a four."

Jonathan scoffed and jumped out of the boat. Renee chose to use the steps.

Jonathan ran his fingers through his mane, causing his tattoos to flex with the movement. Renee realized she had left her bag on the ship and was about to turn to retrieve it when he grabbed her hand.

She gasped as he pulled her body close to him. His face inches away, his eyes staring hungrily at her lips. Before he could speak, Renee nervously pushed him away and stepped back to give herself room. Unfortunately, she misjudged the size of the dock space behind her.

She fell backward into the water with a splash. It all happened so suddenly that she couldn't even scream. Bobbing back to the surface, she coughed out the salt water, her hair matted to her face, arms flailing wildly to keep herself afloat.

Jonathan was beside her in a flash, grabbing her to assist her to the back of the ship and guiding her up the ladder. Shakily, she climbed to the dock, her white dress plastered against her body. Her sandals were lost, leaving her barefoot. Renee felt exposed under the now transparent garment.

Embarrassed by her fall, she panicked and fled across the street and back to her hotel before Jonathan even placed his feet on the wooden boards.

3

———————

Her bare feet slapped against the cold tile of the lobby. She walked toward the elevator, and every step was a reminder of the humiliating fall. She stopped mid-stride, quickly realizing she had left her bag on the ship. Renee groaned with frustration.

Turning to the front desk, she walked shamefully to the concierge. He was a tall older gentleman, thin, with a pointed nose.

His expression proved to Renee that she looked like an absolute mess. "Miss, are you alright?"

"I lost my room key. And do not have my ID," she explained, trying to force confidence in her voice.

"Of course, let me get you another and perhaps a towel?" he said sympathetically.

"That would be wonderful," she said.

As Renee waited, he handed her a white cotton towel, and she dried off her face and arms. She wrapped the cloth around her body to cover herself. Handing Renee the key, the doorman smiled.

"Is there anything else I can assist you with?" he asked.

"Is your lounge open for lunch?" she asked. Her stomach was

suddenly growling with hunger, famished from all the activities. She had not eaten because of her nerves.

"I am sorry, we open for dinner only," he said, "but there is a restaurant next door, and it is highly recommended."

"Does it have a bar?" she asked.

"Yes," he replied, smirking.

"Good," she said and stormed off to her room, forgetting to thank him.

Renee took her time getting ready. A hot shower and fresh clothes lightened her dark mood. She styled her hair and slipped on a clean pair of capris and a tank top, hanging the drenched sundress on the shower rod to dry.

She was grateful the hotel was so close, and she did not have to retreat far looking like a drowned raccoon. The mascara running dark circles under her eyes must have been a sight for the locals.

She slipped on a pair of sneakers and ventured out to the suggested eatery next door. The sign was large, and she was shocked she had missed it, walking by it a few times now.

Captains Cove Bar and Grille was a typical tourist trap. It had an enormous wrap-around tiki bar with neon beer signs and coconut glassware. The servers were all wearing short sailor uniforms, and the bartender had a captain's hat on his head. The dining room was full of people eating pleasantly, and the happy crowd echoed through the establishment.

Renee approached the bar, which was nearly empty due to the early afternoon hour. She sat down on the stool and exhaled. Letting her discomfort slip away.

"Ahoy!" the captain said to her kindly. "We are running a two-for-one special on rum runners and blue lagoons."

Renee smiled. "Perfect. Pick one and a menu, please."

The bartender's smile started to fade. "Rough morning?"

He pulled out a menu and placed it next to her.

"I'd rather not dive into it," she answered. Renee sneered at her quip.

She glanced down at the extravagant list of specials and entrees as he prepared her drink. The menu looked to be four pages long. Distracted, she flipped through carelessly.

"Do you have a favorite sandwich?" she asked, changing the subject.

"Yes, I-" he started, but Renee interrupted with a grin.

"I will take it," she said.

He shook her cocktail and nodded compliantly. Renee glanced around the restaurant, then returned her gaze to the server. He placed an obnoxious coconut in front of her, garnished with pirate flags carved out of pineapple slices and other fruits.

Renee frowned and rolled her eyes.

"Some drink you got there," Jonathan grumbled in her ear.

Renee felt her body tense at the intrusion. She moaned out in disbelief.

"Jonathan!" the bartender shouted from across the room.

"Hey Bill, I will have what she's having, eighty-six the fruit,"

Captain Bill smiled and returned to work as Jonathan settled on the barstool beside her. Renne watched as the blue drink was poured into a pint glass and slid to him.

Jonathan looked at Renee and smirked.

"Here, allow me," he traded drinks with her and lifted the giant coconut to toast, "to new friends making a splash."

Renee shook her head but lifted the glass to meet his fruit-filled orb.

"I am so embarrassed," she said, taking a drink.

The concoction was sweet, not her usual choice. Jonathan struggled with his coconut and pushed it away after tasting it.

Bill returned suddenly with a turkey club and glanced at their discarded beverages.

"Bill, I do not know what the hell that is, but I can not drink that shit," Jonathan laughed, "two beers, please."

Renee was grateful for his honesty and quickly devoured a quarter of the sandwich. She pushed the plate towards Jonathan, and he accepted.

Taking a bite, he spoke with his mouth full, reminding Renee again of his youth.

"You ran off in such a hurry I did not think I would see you again," he said, wiping his mouth with the back of his hand.

Renee slid a napkin to him out of habit.

"How did you find me here?" she asked suspiciously, sipping her beer.

"I was just popping over for lunch," he said, putting the sandwich down and taking a long drink, "when I get here, I always scan the bar for beautiful women sitting alone."

Renee could feel her cheeks redden. "You have to stop with that talk."

"What talk?" he said, placing his hand close to hers.

She retreated, grabbing more of the sandwich and eating quickly.

Jonathan chuckled at her reaction, grabbed the napkin, and wiped his mouth.

"I would love to show you around the island if you wanted," he said.

"I don't know," she said, swallowing her drink. His flirting made her second guess her judgment, and she hurried through her lunch, hopeful of retreating to her room.

She went to grab her purse to pay and groaned loudly.

"Oh no," she said, horrified at her stupidity.

"What is it?" he asked, concerned.

"My bag is on your boat," she said, "and my cards are in my bag."

Jonathan pulled out his wallet and threw money on the bar, much more than the amount of the tab.

"Lunch is on me," he said, "if you would please join me today for the inland tour."

Renee shifted in her seat, weighing her options.

"Come on, I am not dangerous; I have saved your life twice," he joked.

After a long pause, she finally agreed.

Jonathan's face lit up like a kid on Christmas morning. He rose from his stool and held out his hand. Renee stared at him cautiously.

"Thank you for lunch," she said, brushing off his gesture, "I will pay you back."

"Absolutely not," he said, placing his hand on the small of her back and guiding her out of the restaurant.

Renee felt uneasy with his palm on her body but moved quickly outside to the open space. She began walking down the strip when she realized Jonathan was not following her.

"Where are you going?" he asked, standing by the exit.

"I thought you were showing me the island?" she asked.

"I am. Come this way," he waved his hand and motioned her to the parking lot adjacent to the building.

Renee sighed and followed him. Jonathan stopped in front of a black motorcycle detailed in chrome.

"What is this?" she asked, regretting her decision to join him.

"This is the best way to see the strip," Jonathan beamed.

"I do not ride on motorcycles," she said, backing away.

"Or jet skis or boats," he said sarcastically.

"These things are dangerous," she replied.

"Trust me," Jonathan said, lifting his leg over the bike and kicking up the stand, "hop on."

All self-reservation boiled up and over her, leaving little fight left. This was another adventure she would have never embarked on at home. A voice deep inside was edging her on. *Take the chance and risk a little.*

She climbed on the back of the machine and did her best not to get too close to Jonathan's body. It was nearly impossible.

"Now, the safest way to travel," he started to explain, leaning back into her, "is closer to the driver."

He placed his hands under her thighs and pulled her tightly to his waist. He then grabbed her arms without glancing back and wrapped her around his torso. Renee could feel the tight muscles underneath his shirt.

She held her breath as the seat rumbled to life. Renee clutched Jonathan's shirt tightly at the intrusive sound. Her entire body was rigid from nerves.

"Relax," he said, shifting the bike and pulling out of the restaurant.

Stopping at the exit, he looked for oncoming traffic, and Renee took a moment to say a short prayer.

"How long have you been riding?" Renee asked, trying to do the math in her head.

"I just got the bike last week," he answered.

"What?" she shouted over the rip of the engine.

Jonathan laughed and sped down the open street, Renee holding him firmly, wondering what the hell she was thinking.

4

The street was bustling with tourists. Everyone was out shopping, and there were live bands on each street corner, with crowds of people congregating to cheer them on. The bright colors of the buildings set against the baby blue cloudless sky looked like a blur as they traveled fast down the street.

Renee closed her eyes and felt the warm air on her face. As she clung to the young man in front of her, she had to admit she was having fun.

Never having ridden on a motorcycle before, Renee was skittish at first. As Jonathan weaved in and out of traffic, she could feel herself start to relax. Her body rested gently on his back, and her hands felt looser around his waist. When he stopped at the traffic light, he placed his left hand over her own, letting it rest gently on her skin. Too afraid to let go, she allowed him the gesture.

"There are a lot of things to do all over the island," he said to her over the noise of the busy street.

She nodded, forgetting that he couldn't see her. He squeezed her hand.

"I didn't lose you back there, did I?" he asked playfully.

Renee cleared her throat and answered. "Sorry, I am just trying to take it all in."

"I am going to bring you to my favorite spot on the island, it is a little bit of a ride, but it is worth the trip," he said, bringing his hand back to the bar as the light turned green.

Renee had no choice but to ride behind him. She was at the mercy of whatever Jonathan had decided to do on their adventure. She watched the sidewalks while he navigated on. He was occasionally pointing out different landmarks and popular spots.

Renee noticed the buildings were starting to spread out. There were fewer people on this end of the island. She wondered where on earth Jonathan was headed as the sun started its slow descent toward the horizon.

Jonathan pulled up to a large green sign reading *Galveston Seawall* and parked the bike. He stretched his arms over his head and let out a loud sigh. Renee was not sure what to do, so she sat awkwardly, awaiting his instructions.

Laughing, he grabbed her hands from his waist and unclasped them. "There, we made it in one piece."

"Thank goodness," she huffed.

He helped her dismount, and she stood, adjusting her outfit. Jonathan looked around, smiling, lifting both arms in the air to present his destination proudly.

"Welcome to Galveston Seawall," he said.

"Thanks," she replied, unsure of what was so special about a barrier.

Jonathan could sense the doubt in her voice, and a look of disappointment flashed over his face.

"Come with me," he said and walked determined toward the path.

She followed him down the stone walkway and approached a mile marker.

"It is a two-mile walk round trip, but we can make good time; I am glad you wore sneakers," he said and glanced down at her feet.

Renee was left bewildered at what Jonathan was intending, but the two started walking down the broken path.

"This is Galveston's historic sea wall," he explained; his pace was hurried, forcing Renee to speed up her cadence. "It is ten miles long and was built after a hurricane in 1900."

"Ten miles?" she asked hesitantly.

"We are only walking part of it," he said, "the best part."

Renee continued as Jonathan picked up his history lesson. He knew a lot about the area and had a passion for storytelling. Renee admired his outgoing and friendly personality. She understood why he was in the boat touring business. It came naturally to him.

His exterior screamed bad boy, the way his hair was long and needed a trim, blowing wildly in the sea breeze. His arms covered in tattoos put her off earlier, but upon closer inspection seemed to all be strategically placed. He had a portrait of King Neptune on his tricep, sitting atop a monstrous wave; there was a squid or octopus below him, wrapping his tentacles down around his body, attempting to drag him into the water. The rest of the artwork was not visible under his shirt, and Renee had vaguely remembered what was on the other side. She was not a big fan of tattoos, but on Jonathan, they were fitting.

She was reminiscing on how she was forced to straddle herself around him to get here, and the tension in her stomach returned. She could still smell his aftershave as she walked steadily behind him. Suddenly, Jonathan stopped short, and she collided with his back, making him stumble forward.

"I'm sorry," she said, grabbing his arm to steady him.

Jonathan stood straight and looked down at her arm, the corners of his mouth turned upward slowly.

"We are here," he said in a low voice, taking her hand and pulling her to a railing.

Renee looked around, there were a few people scattered along the shoreline below, and a couple of kids were throwing a frisbee on the beach. There was nothing but the stone wall and a large metal fence separating them from the ocean. Renee turned around and looked back toward the strip.

"What are we looking at?" she asked, confused.

Jonathan grabbed her by the hips and pulled her close. She could feel her heartbeat faster in her chest. He moved his lips to graze her ear and whispered onto her neck. The sensation sent a shiver up her spine.

He used his body to guide her around, facing the ocean once more. "This."

The sky was on fire with the most vibrant orange and reds Renee had ever seen. The blue ocean underneath looked like a never-ending quilt of diamonds, adorned by the sparkling white pattern that twinkled with the incoming tide. The way the sun melted down into the horizon was like watching butter on a stack of pancakes, spreading the warmth across the sky.

As the sun set low, the people below them slowly turned to black silhouettes. The view swept Renee away, and she held her breath in awe. She forgot that Jonathan's arms were still positioned on her hips, her back resting leisurely on his chest.

When he shifted his weight, she regained her senses and stepped forward towards the rail. To her dismay, Jonathan quickly followed, resting his hands on either side of her.

"It is stunning," he whispered again.

"Absolutely gorgeous," she said.

Jonathan released the rail, and Renee exhaled. She was finding it hard to catch her breath around him. The sun disappeared under the water, and the sky remained a glowing orange.

"My father used to say this was how the heavens kissed the earth," Jonathan said, facing the magnificent view.

"That's beautiful," Renee said, taken back by the poetic sentiment.

The air was cooling as the burning sky also faded; they stood and watched the night creep in.

Jonathan clapped his hands loudly and spun around. "We should get back."

Renee chuckled at his energy. They strolled along the walkway, Renee asking more about his father. Jonathan explained how he passed away from cancer.

"It's the worst way to go," he said sadly, "slow and painful. People are lucky to punch out quickly from an accident. Those people skip the pain and suffering of old age or disease that haunt you at the end."

Renee studied him in the lamplight. This was the most serious she had witnessed him since they met. The relationship he had with his father was exceptionally strong and loving.

"I'm sorry,'" she said.

"It's alright," he looked at her, his eyes glowing.

As they approached the bike, she felt better about climbing on the back. More comfortable than before. The sunset stroll was an unexpected stop, and she appreciated the unusual sightseeing. If anyone had asked her a few days ago if she would have followed a stranger on a two-mile walk to a secluded pier to watch a stunning sunset, she would have laughed at them.

So far, her trip had been more adventurous than she had ever expected, all after meeting the young man she held onto during the ride back.

He must be twenty years younger. She thought to herself, attempting to bury the feelings she had been ignoring all along.

He was so charming and caring. Different from her ex and other interests in almost every way. Renee was curious to know if doubt was the right feeling to have or caution.

She struggled with the creeping desire and gripped his waist tighter. The friction of their bodies only makes it harder. Jonathan shifted the bike and moved faster down the street, the buildings and lights flying by them in a blur. He pulled the bike over onto the side of the street and turned it off.

"Where are we now?" she asked, confused.

"The night is still young, and I am thirsty," he said, getting off he turned to Renee, "there are many more sights to see at nightfall."

Winking at Renee, she hesitantly joined him on the curb.

"Why do I feel like this is a bad idea?" she asked, fixing her hair and pulling down her tank.

"Have I steered you wrong so far?" he laughed, grabbing her hand.

Renee could hear the music blasting out into the night from the different buildings.

"I don't know about this, Jonathan," she said, stepping back toward the street.

He looked at her sadly and made a pouting face. His full lips mock her.

He pulled her close and mumbled low inches from her face. "If you aren't having fun after one drink, I will bring you back to the hotel."

"One drink," she said, eyeing his lips. An unfamiliar desire washed over her body as his face lit up at her response.

5

The reverberation of the club music made the concrete vibrate. People were lining the streets, drinking and shouting at each other. It was like watching a large frat party gathering by the front door of the bar. Lights were flashing from the inside and back decks.

Renee watched the young women dressed in cut-off denim shorts and bikini tops fumble back and forth from bar to bar. Their tan skin was hardly covered, leaving little to the imagination. The women outnumbered the men, three to one on the streets. It was like watching sharks in a sea of mackerel, scouring for the perfect meal.

To say Renee felt out of place would be an understatement. Her outfit was conservative, her hair and makeup plain compared to the sight around her. She was dragged along by Jonathan, who was headed toward the noise and ruckus. One drink would be torture enough for her, and she already couldn't wait to leave.

Jonathan turned to look at her mid-stride. His eyes were wild with the flashing lights; his countenance screamed trouble. Her heart sank, predicting his destination to be the loudest and the most obnoxious choice on the strip.

To Renee's amazement, he strolled past the busy establishment.

The young ladies leaning against the brick walls stared at Jonathan as they made their way through the crowd. Breaking free of the suffocating mob, Renne was led to a softly lit bar tucked back on the corner of the street.

There was a chalkboard sign outside advertising an open mic night. The thumping of house music faded behind them as Jonathan opened a heavy wooden door and motioned her politely inside. The sound of country bluegrass graced her ears while continuing through the entrance.

Looking around, she noticed there were wooden booths set in charming rustic decor. Decorated in iron and wood, the inside of the bar reminded her of back home in Austin, which was known for its music. This bar had autographed pictures of musicians lining the walls, postcards, and dollar bills scattered behind the bar.

Renee smiled, thankful for Jonathan's choice of venue. There were very few scandalous outfits inside, and Renee immediately felt more comfortable. One beer would taste much better here.

"Bar or booth?" the hostess asked them as they reached the podium.

"Bar," Jonathan said loudly over the music.

She nodded and let them pass. He approached the long wooden counter and chose two stools nestled in the corner.

Renee sat closer to the wall; her vantage point allowed her to view the entire room. Jonathan sat eagerly down and turned to her breathless.

"This place has live music just about every night," he said.

"I like it," she said, smiling.

Jonathan gazed at her proudly. "Those clubs aren't my style."

They ordered their drinks, Jonathan a beer and Renne a vodka martini. Renee shuddered when the bartender asked to see Jonathan's ID and not her own. Jonathan handed it over without a second thought, while Renee's conscience brought her back to their obvious age gap.

"You are full of surprises," she said, lifting her martini and taping her glass to his.

"We just met; imagine what revelations you will discover in time," he smirked at her.

Renee shifted her eyes to the man on stage, singing a cover of a Johnny Cash song.

"Well, you better get to talking if I am going to learn anything more," she smiled out into the room, "the deal was one drink remember?"

Jonathan set the glass down and chuckled. "The lawyer doesn't mess around."

"No, I do not; you're lucky I haven't put the deal in writing," she joked.

Her sudden softness awed the young man, who had spent the last two days trying desperately to lighten her spirits. In the laid-back atmosphere, she was starting to really feel like she was on vacation.

"Tell me more about this agreement you have with your coworkers," he said, "you have to provide proof of fun or something?"

Renee sipped her cold martini, the lemon peel bumping into her lips.

"Well, it's kind of a long story," she said.

"We have time," Jonathan motioned to his full glass.

Renee proceeded to explain her situation and how she had been married for nineteen years to a very successful defense lawyer. How the couple met in the courtroom, fell in love, and jumped into marriage.

As she spoke to Jonathan about her past, the martini dwindled, and he motioned for another. Bringing up her troubles made her thirsty, and she did not argue when the fresh beverage was placed in front of her.

Renee spoke about how, in the beginning, things were great. They were two passionate personalities, consumed by their careers. They never wanted children, thank goodness, that would have made everything much more difficult. Renee did not regret the decision until later when she noticed how empty her life felt. How distant her relationship with her husband had become.

She was working out of town and planned to stay an extra night to avoid the rushed flight. She had called home and left a message, informing her then-husband of her travel plans. They rarely spoke directly on the phone and only saw each other in passing when they were under the same roof.

Her plans changed suddenly when her colleague introduced her to a new client, who had his own private plane, and a large bankroll. Along with the flight home came a business opportunity she couldn't pass up. So she used the six hours to talk shop and land the account.

Arriving home a day early, Renne walked quietly inside the house. She set her luggage in the foyer like she had done countless times before. There was something strange this time. She discovered an open wine bottle on the counter and poured herself a glass.

Sipping it and ascending the staircase to the bedroom, excited to take a shower and wash the trip off of her skin.

There were two messages on the machine, but she chose to shower first. She remembered the bathroom was a mess. Patrick was usually more relaxed while she was out of town. It looked like he had left the house in a hurry that morning. Once exiting the shower, she wrapped herself in a clean towel and picked up her glass. She pressed play on the machine and casually searched her dresser for some clothes.

The first message was her own, including the information about her departure time. She noticed how cold her voice was over the recording. Renee wondered when that warmth had faded over the last two decades. She had pulled out a pair of sweats and threw them on the bed, taking a large gulp of wine.

The second message started. It was a nurse at the local emergency room trying to reach Patrick's emergency contact. He was in an accident and admitted to the hospital. She was told to come immediately. Renee spit out her wine. It erupted over her bedspread like splattered paint. Her clothes were stained red, reminding her of blood and making her feel faint.

She only remembers a little about getting dressed. Her hair was still wet, and her shoes did not match when she stormed into the hospital entrance. She had barked at the receptionists about her husband's name and date of birth. The look on the woman's face was perplexed, which irritated Renee.

She made a nasty comment about her inadequacy and marched down the hall to his room number, informed that he was in a coma and already had the maximum number of visitors in the room. The nurse must have been mistaken; the pair had no family left.

When she barreled through the door, she slammed hard into a stranger that was hovering over the bed. It was a teenage boy, his face covered in acne and shock.

There was a blonde woman sitting on Patrick's bed, her face covered in tears. She had a large diamond band on her left hand, similar to Renee's. Their expressions were mirrored, confusion, panic, and pain.

It took Renee only a short time to put the pieces together. With Patrick lying motionless and the teenager beside him, she could tell immediately who the boy was. Little had to be said to the strange woman, but she decided to say it anyway.

"Are you his wife?" she spat at her.

The blonde nodded, the wonderment spread across her pretty face.

"I see," she said.

Renne walked to the bedside table, the boy retreating to his mother's side to get out of her path.

She wrote a note on the pad, folded it, and placed it in Patrick's wallet that sat alongside their comatose husband. She snickered at the ironic sight, hoping he would live so that she could kill him herself.

Renee looked up at the two strangers and frowned. "I want you to know I am very sorry."

She turned and walked out the door, never to see the sister's wife and bastard son again.

6

———————

Jonathan's mouth hung open as she concluded her tale. Renee finished her drink and placed the empty glass next to the other two. Her guard was down, and she worried she may have overshared her difficult past.

Jonathan motioned for another round, but Renee stopped the bartender, asking for water instead.

"How about a light beer?" Jonathan suggested.

She nodded and waited for the drinks to be served.

"That sounds like a made-for-television movie," he said once they were alone.

"Unfortunately, it does," she agreed.

"So it was a double life?" he asked, trying to clarify.

"Yeah, apparently, he dropped them off to park the car while they were together and got into a bad accident, resulting in a coma," she explained.

"We don't need to talk about this if it is upsetting," Jonathan said, concerned.

"No, I am okay," she took a sip of the pale lager.

"Good, because I have one more question," Jonathan leaned in.

Renee raised her eyebrow and waited.

"What was on the note you left for him?"

Renee chuckled and spoke slowly. "Lustitiae servitium est."

"What the fuck does that mean?" he said, befuddled.

"It is something that we used to say to each other after winning a big case," she explained, "a Latin toast that means justice has been served."

"Wow," Jonathan sat back on his barstool. His shoulders sank down as he appeared lost in thought.

"I'm sorry for killing the mood," she said, staring down into her glass.

"You should not apologize for what that asshole did to you," he said quickly, putting his arm behind her chair.

Renee felt trapped in the corner of the bar, Jonathan's large frame blocking her from the rest of the room.

"So the trip was to prove I can still have fun and that the best years of my life haven't passed me by," Renee continued, ignoring his hand that was brushing her back lightly.

Jonathan laughed at her. "Your best years, you aren't even close."

Renee raised another brow at him and frowned. "I am flattered, but yes, I am close, and second chances of love don't just fall from the sky."

Jonathan looked at her quizzically.

Renee realized she had blurted out the wrong word. "Life, I meant life."

The stage at the back of the bar picked up the tempo as a new artist began singing a fun country song. Jonathan turned toward the music and then back to Renee, rising from his stool.

She was shaking her head in refusal, but it didn't matter. Grabbing her hand tightly, he pulled her off the stool and dragged her to the center of the open dance floor. There were a few people dancing on the edges while Jonathan decided on center stage.

She stood there, uncomfortable, while he rocked back and forth on his feet. Feeling like a fish out of water watching the others laugh and have fun stepping around in unison. Jonathan noticed her lack of participation and moved closer to her, grinding his hips against her side.

The martinis had loosened her witts, and she let out a giggle, which only pushed him to continue. Jonathan raised up his strong arms and snapped his fingers to the beat blasting out of the speakers. Renee decided that standing stoic was more awkward than caving in. She moved her body rigidly to the music.

Dissatisfied with her efforts, Jonathan stepped behind her and placed his hands on her hips. He was using his strength to pull her closer to him and guide her body to the beat. The sensation of his torso against her back felt safe. Renee allowed herself to get lost for a moment in his arms. Right before she closed her eyes, her body twirled around quickly, and Jonathan grabbed her hands, leading them in a fast-paced two-step.

The people in the booths around seemed to gravitate toward the floor like magnets. Soon there were multiple couples dancing and enjoying themselves. Renee was stealing a glimpse of the room, but Jonathan's eyes were locked on her, burning like the sunset they had shared only hours before.

She smiled at him, ready to admit she was having fun.

"You should do that more often," he shouted over the music.

"What?" she asked him, stumbling over his feet.

Jonathan caught her and brought her back upright, laughing.

"Smile," he answered. "I would do anything for that smile."

Renee blushed and started to back away, but Jonathan held fast and twirled her around.

They continued to dance until sweat started to form on her forehead. She wanted to retreat to the bar and grab a drink at the lull in the music. When a new artist took the stage, they started back. They were busy laughing when a slow tempo filled the room. Jonathan put his hand on her shoulder, causing her to stop in her tracks.

He lifted his hand to her waist and drew her small frame to his chest. Renee placed her hand on his muscular bicep and moved closer. His lips parted, realizing she was not fighting him this time. Jonathan looked down, studying her face. She could feel the warmth of his breath on her skin. The smell of the sea lingered in his wild hair as they danced slowly across the floor.

The bar disappeared while rocking against Jonathan. Renee felt like they were the only two people in the room. The way he looked at her made something deep inside rumble and stir. Feelings that she had not felt for such a long time were creeping their way to the surface.

A smile snuck back on her lips. Jonathan's lips were pursed together tightly. He looked as if he was struggling to say something.

Finally, he leaned in and whispered in her ear. "Second chances of love may not fall from the sky, but rather rescue us from the deepest of waters when we feel helpless and lost."

Renee let his words resonate as they continued their dance. She was resting her head on his strong chest and absorbing the feeling of being held by his charm.

The song ended, and she broke their embrace.

"I need a drink," she said and used the excuse to flee back to the bar.

The bartender announced it was the last call as she finished her beer. "We should be getting back."

Jonathan nodded in agreement and paid the tab.

When they emerged outside, there were people stumbling all throughout the street. Jonathan grabbed her hand and pulled her away from his bike.

"Let's walk," he said, smiling, "I have been drinking and do not want to risk it."

Renne was relieved by his responsible decision. He assured her it was only a few blocks from the hotel, and they walked together in the moonlight.

Renee chatted pleasantly, but her mind raced with thoughts.

When they approached the hotel, Jonathan stopped and ran his fingers through his hair. He looked nervous under the lamp light.

"Thank you for a wonderful day," she said, looking down at her hands.

Jonathan stepped closer and placed his finger under her chin, drawing her face up to meet his eyes.

His lips landed on hers in a hurry, hard and firm, with an incredible hunger. Renee could not stifle the moan that escaped her body, causing him to push her into the brick wall behind them.

It may have been the drinks, the fresh ocean air, or the persistence she had been fighting since they met. It did not matter what it was; Renee closed her eyes and let Jonathan explore her mouth with his tongue. His large hands traveled to her hips, and his body was pressed firmly against her.

He groaned into her. Letting his mouth travel to the nape of her neck, the soft trail of kisses sent an electric current through her body. His hands squeezed her skin in response to her reaction. Renee could feel the excitement protruding from his hips.

A car full of young kids went zooming by, shouting at the couple. Embarrassed by her public display, she quickly pushed Jonathan away and stepped closer to the door.

"I can't," she said, flustered.

He stared at her. His mouth opened in protest, but he was unable to find the words.

"You are so sweet, but this is not right; I can't," she repeated.

His eyes softened their intense stare, and he started closer.

"You are so young, don't waste your efforts on me," she stuttered and reached for the handle.

Jonathan frowned, and before he could answer, Renee yanked open the door and retreated into the hotel.

When she stepped into the elevator, she could still see him staring at her from the window. The metal doors closed on his hurt expression.

7

———

Sleep did not come at all that night. Dizzy from the drinks but drunker on Jonathan's kisses, Renee was left to stare at the ceiling of her hotel room. Her body was wired as if she had stuck her finger in an electrical socket. No matter how hard she shook her head, the thoughts of the evening kept invading her mind.

Renee rolled around on the bed uncomfortably, angry at herself and her behavior. She would have never kissed a stranger back home. This was totally uncharacteristic.

The hotel room felt cramped.

She searched for a distraction, anything to take her mind off of the passionate encounter from moments ago. Buzzed from the evening's events, she foolishly scoured the room for her cell phone.

As humility washed over her body, the realization of her phone's location sank in. Walking to the window, she stared across the street at the large tour and rental sign.

A light was on outside, and Jonathan's boat was visible, beckoning her. Renee stood and contemplated her options.

She could wait and grab her phone in the morning, but she would have to face him again, possibly. After the sudden rejection, she preferred not to experience any more uncomfortable situations.

Renee crossed her arms over her chest and exhaled. The glass exposed her mirrored reflection. At first, she did not recognize the woman staring back at her. Even with her aggravated state, her expression seemed softer. There was a light in her eye that she hadn't seen in years. The excitement of the trip had changed her somehow. She knew it was solely Jonathan's efforts that had broken down her walls.

She paced the floor, thinking about the unexpected connection they shared. How, when his lips met hers, she was able to put aside his age and enjoy the rush. Renee cursed herself for always ruining these moments with her logic and wondered if this was what she needed to start fresh. A master of self-sabotage, she needed to break the pattern of unhappiness that stalked her life.

What happened with her ex-husband may seem astonishing to most, but Renee would be lying if she admitted she did not see it coming. The two had grown so far apart, like strangers living as roommates for years, she suffered through the daily grind of being a housewife, giving up the thoughts of love and passion somewhere along the way.

There was no time for self-pity or moping around. She took the trip reluctantly and wanted it over quickly so she could return to work. Jonathan was pleasant company and outside her plan.

Renee made her decision. Slipping on her sneakers, she once again fled the hotel to sneak onto the ship and retrieve her things and told herself she should avoid Jonathan for the rest of the trip.

The night air invaded her senses as she stepped out into the street. The moon was low; daylight was only a few hours away.

Jogging across the empty road and approaching the rental building, Renne scanned the area for anyone watching. The coast seemed clear, and she made her way down the long dock to the ship. The sounds of the waves were her only companion.

Renee stepped carefully down onto the deck, it was dark even with the pale moonlight, and she had to duck down low to search for her bag, praying it was still where she had left it.

The fiberglass felt cool to the touch.

The boat suddenly started, sending the floor into a slow vibration. Renee knelt horrified, aware that she was not actually alone after all. A man cleared his throat behind her, causing Renee to jolt to her feet.

"Wait!" she shouted from the bow at the silhouette behind the helm.

It was too late. The boat was pulling away quickly from the dock.

Jonathan's shocked expression was brief as he stumbled backward and tripped over a cooler behind him, sending him backward over the rail. In an instant, he disappeared, and the sound of the splash exploded into the night.

Renee ran to the edge, trying to figure out what to do next.

"Cut the engine!" he screamed, coughing up the salt water.

Renee ran to the controls. She was staring dumbfounded at the different knobs and gauges and cursing at herself for being so foolish. Finally spotting a key, she turns it quickly, and the engine makes a terrible grinding sound before going silent.

The sound of the man swimming to the boat filled the air. Renee sat down on the seat and held her head with her shaking hands.

"What the hell are you doing here?" Jonathan emerged from the ladder, soaking wet. His shorts were pooling water on the deck.

"I was coming for my things," she stuttered, "I was going to grab them and leave, I swear."

Jonathan brought both of his hands to his hair, pulling it back to ring out. His face was full of fury, making Renee's insides fill with regret.

"You shouldn't have been sneaking around in the dark," he said, "I would have brought you the things in the morning."

"I am sorry; I didn't expect you to be here; I didn't want to have to bother you again," she said in a somber tone.

Jonathan inspected the controls as the boat drifted out to sea; turning it over, he let it idle. The way he studied the craft was like caring for a sick child. Renee felt guilty for any damage she may have caused and stood to ensure she hadn't broken anything.

"Did I break it?" she asked, concerned.

He refused to meet her eyes and continued tweaking the controls. "I have to let it idle to make sure, but it looks fine."

Renee nodded. "I feel like a fool."

Jonathan's chest deflated, and he stared out into the open water.

"Listen, I am sorry, I will pay for anything that-" she began.

"That's not it," he said to her, annoyed.

"Then what is it?" she answered.

"You would rather sneak over her undetected than see me again?" he said, the hurt thick in his voice.

Renee looked down at her feet and was at a loss for words.

"I don't get it, Renee," he continued, "what is it about me that isn't good enough for you?"

She looked up, shocked, "Jonathan, whatever gave you that impression?"

He stepped closer to her and hovered, drops of water dripping down upon her dry shirt.

"You haven't been very easy to read," he said.

"You are too young to understand," she said, "I don't want to lead you on; there could be no future in this."

Jonathan pulled the boat neutral and turned off the engine. He dropped anchor with the flip of a switch. Turning to her and grabbing the back of her neck, he pulled her forehead to his own, his lips inches from hers. She stared longingly into his persistent eyes.

"You are stubborn, but I am old enough to make my own decisions Renee,"

Renee could not stand the tension any longer. She placed her hands on his wet chest and pursed her lips against him in a long sensual kiss. Whatever reserves she held dissolved as the yearning inside her took over, granting Jonathan permission to proceed at last.

His hands wandered over her body, his heat emanating onto her skin. For just taking a dunk in the chilly sea, he was surprisingly warm.

His hands reached around her back and rested around her hips. Using his strength, he lifted her up, draping her legs around his body, using his right arm to cradle her, his left arm to press her back firmly into him.

Descending the cabin stairs effortlessly, he brought his mouth back to her chest, peppering her skin with kisses, and Renee leaned her head back, soaking in the sensation. Opening her eyes, she scanned her surroundings. The small living space had a few essentials, but Jonathan's destination was the queen size mattress at the back of the den.

Setting her down gently and backing away, she studied his body, glistening from the light shining through the small window placed high on the wall. He peeled off his wet clothing and went to work on Renee next. She lay there absorbing his touch, becoming lost in his arms as the bed underneath her rocked steadily with the ocean waves.

8

———————

Johnathan sighed and stretched, bringing his arms to wrap tightly around the gorgeous woman next to him. He kissed her bare neck, and she shivered at his touch. Smiling, he traveled further down her slender neck. Renee sat up quickly and turned to him with a sly grin. Her cautious expression forced him to halt his second advance. Wrapping their bodies in sheets, they emerged from the cabin to a blazing sunrise. Renee stared at the sight in wonder.

"I have shared a sunset and sunrise with you already," he said, wrapping his strong arms around her waist and kissing her shoulder gently.

"This is not how I usually operate," she said playfully.

"I figured," he whispered, squeezing her slender frame.

Jonathan closed his eyes and breathed in the scent of her hair. Her presence calmed his racing mind. It seemed like fate acted, leaving the phone on the ship, drawing the woman back at just the right time. He was so flustered with the evening's end that he had decided to go fishing. The fish bite better in the early hours of the morning, right before sunrise. What he caught instead was much more satisfying.

He watched her as she walked forward and leaned against the rail, looking like a goddess in the white sheet. Her hair blew lightly in the refreshing breeze. He had to look away; his attraction to the woman was hard to control. Not wanting to push his luck, he returned to the berth and grabbed his shorts. Yanking them on quickly, he turned to join Renee.

She had followed him down the stairs quietly; he did not notice she was standing in the doorframe. He bumped into her, and she started to fall backward. Catching her at the waist, she threw her arms around his neck and clung to him.

His eyes must have given his thoughts away. Renee stood, leaving her body draped around his neck, and twirled his hair in her fingers. She kissed him, closing her eyes and pushing herself close to him. The sheet fell to the floor, and the woman stood naked before him.

"You are not very agile, are you, Renee?" He said as his lips met the flesh under her chin.

"My sea legs are weak," she giggled into the air.

He traveled across her chest, soaking in every inch of her tan skin. She tasted like honey and sea salt—no doubt from their surroundings.

"If we continue this, we will be stuck on this barge all day," she joked.

"I have food and water if it comes to that," he whispered against her skin.

Just then, a fog horn blasted loudly from the stern, making them both jump.

Jonathan released Renee, and she moved aside to allow him to climb the stairs quickly. The anchor had broken free, and they were drifting into the busy channel. Angry seamen were shouting at him, and he waved his apologies. Jonathan steered his boat across the water towards the safety of the dock.

Renee appeared fully clothed. She was holding his shirt in her hand. Reaching out to give it to him, he hesitated to accept.

"The captain requests you return to the cabin Miss," he said, disappointed.

Shaking her head, she laughed. "I believe this voyage is over."

"Or it has only just begun," he said, winking. The ship pulled up to the dock with ease. "Let's grab breakfast."

She nodded her approval. "This time, I will buy."

He didn't protest. Jonathan was pleased she was slower to run away. Renee seemed to accept that the two could have some harmless fun together.

Tying off the boat and unloading his precious cargo, he strolled into the office where Chris had just started the work day.

"Hey, boss," he said cheerily, "you're here early."

Jonathan grinned. "Yes, and leaving for the day."

Chris looked up and noticed Renee. His smirk was faint, but the boy understood.

"Don't worry about things here; I got it under control,"

Jonathan led Renee to the motorcycle he had retrieved while she had run off to her room. Starting it up and letting it idle.

Renee shouted over his shoulder. "Do you know a good breakfast spot?"

"The best," he answered and pulled the bike carefully into traffic.

"Great, I am starving," she said into his ear.

The day was hot already as he weaved them through town. They were passing the bars and restaurants on each side and making their way to the outskirts of the main strip. Johnathan pulled into a dirt driveway, the dust and rocks kicking up as he continued toward the ocean's shore. His beach house stood before them.

"Where are we?" she asked from behind him.

He pulled the bike under the carport and shut it off. "Consider it a Bed and Breakfast."

Jonathan went to unlock the door before she could remark and stepped inside. His home was an older bungalow with large dormer windows and a spacious loft. He made his way to the kitchen and opened the refrigerator. Pulling out a carton of eggs, he glanced at Renee, who was lingering in the doorway and looking around.

"Stay a while," he chuckled and walked up to her. He was reaching behind to shut the screen door.

Renee walked into the kitchen and sat at the counter. Jonathan did not own a table; there was no need for it. He often dined alone or in town.

"How do you like your eggs?" he asked. "Scrambled or poached?"

"Over easy," she answered.

"I'm no Bobby Flay," he laughed, waving a spatula at her.

He grabbed an egg and smashed it on the counter, it splattered, and the eggshells broke apart in the pan.

Renee smiled and gave him a look of distaste, rising from her stool and approaching the mess. She took his dish towel and wiped the slime off the surface. Then grabbed the pan and dumped it in the nearby trash.

He stood back and watched her move gracefully in the kitchen. She was pulling out a spatula from a drawer and grabbing the butter from the refrigerator.

"You really know your way around a kitchen," he said, admiring every move.

"I used to cook all the time," she explained, "but then my job got in the way, and I never had the time."

Jonathan felt like she was floating somewhere in a dark memory, so he attempted to pull her back into the room. He brought his hand around her pulling his waist close. She giggled as his hips swayed against her back.

"Don't mess with the chef," she said, waving the utensil behind her.

"Are you prepared to use that as your weapon of choice? Or should I hide my knives?" he laughed.

She grabbed his hand and stuck the rubber in his palm. Closing his fingers around the handle, she leaned in close and whispered.

"The trick with eggs is low and slow," she said.

"Sounds like a method I could manage," he replied.

She blushed and looked at the pan, turning the heat down and allowing the butter to melt.

Jonathan kissed her neck, rubbing his face against her skin. He watched the woman's arms cover in goosebumps from his touch. She cracked an egg and continued her work. She was attempting to ignore his persistence, letting the egg fry in the pan as he peppered her flesh with more kisses.

"Are you paying attention? I am teaching you how to fry an egg," she said; her voice was irritated, but she did not pull away.

"Sure," he lied, letting his hands travel down her sides. Sneaking his hands under her shirt, he felt the warmth of her sun-kissed skin.

With a flip of her wrist, the flash of the yellow yolk flew up into the air and landed upside down on the pan. The sizzle continued as Jonathan's body heated up again. Setting the pan down on the burner, Renee let out a small yelp as he grabbed her hips and lifted her onto the counter. He wasted no time engulfing her in a warm and sensual embrace.

Renee melted faster than the butter on the stove, letting him release her from her top and brush his face against her breasts. He peeled off her shorts and continued his way down her abdomen.

She laid her body back across the counter, spreading her legs open and inviting him closer. Jonathan could smell the egg burning on the stove as smoke began to fill the kitchen.

"Jonathan, the" she started but gasped at the sensation of his mouth against her skin.

He reached over and turned off the burner. He paused only to pick up the skillet and toss it in the sink behind him.

"Breakfast can wait," he said and went back to her trembling knees.

9

The hot water filled the small room with thick steam. The two had been inside long enough for their fingers to prune. They were lost in each other's pleasure with no intention of stopping. They tangled together in the soapy water, and it was hard to see where one body ended and the other began. Like octopi in the sea, they wrapped their limbs together, and much like the male octopus that dies after mating, Jonathan could feel a part of his heart crumble from the thought of losing her.

Jonathan caught Renee's misty eyes and was entranced by her beauty. Vulnerable looked good on her, and he soaked up every stifled sigh, tender touch, and soft whisper.

He would have let the water run forever and dry up the ocean to keep her in his grip. Collapsing onto him, Renee wrapped her slick arms around his neck and passionately attacked his mouth with her own.

"I have never known this feeling could be real," she whispered into his ear over the sounds of splashing water. "The movies always embellish these types of things."

Jonathan grazed his stubble against her chin and spoke to her, "I think it has more to do with chemistry than location."

She reached behind and turned off the faucet, making him groan in disappointment.

"We will grow gills if we stay here any longer," she laughed.

The sound echoed in the small bathroom, sending flutters to Jonathan's chest. He craved that laugh as much as the woman herself.

"Gills would be nice," he said, reaching for the water.

She slapped his hand away playfully and exited the glass door. She was bringing up her hand to rub a big circle in the foggy mirror. Jonathan was shocked at his expression. He almost did not recognize himself. The happiness that radiated off his face was a comforting sight.

The last two days had proven his deep feelings, but he remained reserved. Knowing she would be packing up and leaving soon. He was not one for commitments, and he felt it was ironic that he finally found someone worth keeping, and she existed as a fleeting conquest. Jonathan knew there was little he could do to convince her to stay; he had to enjoy every second of Renee while she was still within reach.

"I have to go back to the hotel and gather my things," she said while tossing him a towel.

He nodded. "You would have saved a fortune on the room if you hadn't fought so hard in the beginning."

He smiled and ran his fingers through his long wet hair. He was placing the towel loosely around his hips. Renee stole a glance at his chiseled torso. She decided to approach him and run her hand down his chest like piano keys. He smiled at her touch, ready to be played again.

She noticed his wicked grin and pulled her hand away. She was bending forward to wring out her hair instead.

"I didn't pay for it," she chuckled. "It was a gift, remember?"

"So I am considered a gift as well?" he said, moving closer to the stunning woman wrapped in his tattered towel.

"You are more of a bonus," she said. "Or an all-inclusive perk."

"I prefer an excursion," he walked forward and grumbled into her hair.

"Whatever you are, I thought you were trouble, but you have proven to be five stars," she smiled.

"Maybe I can talk you into extending your trip?" he said, hopeful.

Jonathan watched Renee's smile fade. The twinkle from her eyes also disappeared, and a pang of sadness spread across her face. It was like watching a curtain of gloom close on the carfree windows of her eyes.

"You know I can't," she said. "My work is waiting. I have a whole life back in Austin."

"You can't blame me for trying," he smiled.

I should have left it alone.

Jonathan tried his best to make her smile and forget about the stress. It seemed too late that the damage had been done. Renee left the bathroom with a dark cloud hovering over her. The thoughts in her mind seemed to pull her away and out of the bedroom. She crossed her arms and stared out of Jonathan's large window. The ocean was on display, crashing against the rocks on the shore. Seagulls were diving from the sky to pick up scraps on the beach.

He walked up behind her and tried to envelop her body in a light hug. Renee pushed him away and fidgeted with her hair. The argument she held with herself was obvious, and Jonathan waited for her to speak.

She inhaled deeply and sunk into the unmade bed. "You knew what this was before it even began."

He watched her intently. She seemed to be speaking more to herself than to Jonathan.

"We have just met, and we are polar opposites," she said, looking around the room. "It is taking everything in me not to start doing laundry or dishes."

Jonathan wanted to laugh, but he felt a twinge of insult in her voice. His apartment was a bachelor's pad; it had not welcomed a woman in months.

"I'm sorry I appear to live in filth," he snapped. Renee looked up quickly from his response.

"That's not what I meant," she said. "You just have a completely different lifestyle. This week was fun, but not a future."

Jonathan's fists clenched, and his teeth ground inside his mouth. "First, I am too young; then I am too reckless; now I am too messy."

Renee looked down at her palms. The towel opened slightly, showing her upper thigh in the bright sunshine. Jonathan walked to his closet and searched around for a clean shirt; the fact he had no clean ones within reach irritated him. He reached down and grabbed a black shirt off the floor, and pulled it on. His shorts were under the bed. He stalked over and retrieved them, ignoring Renee's expression.

"I am sorry; I didn't mean to insult you," Renee said softly.

There was a knock at the front door. Jonathan looked back at her and tried to bite his tongue. His words pushed through his lips before he could control his temper.

"You are right; I am all those things," he said, the hurt apparent in his voice, "But at least I am not too superficial to be happy."

Renee's face was distorted in a hurt expression. He turned quickly to see who was at the door. Kicking things out of his path as he went.

Chris's grin was beaming through the screen door. "Hey, boss!"

His voice was pleasant and excited; Jonathan had to shake the annoyance from his bones before answering the innocent guest.

"Come in," he motioned with his hand.

"You have been a ghost lately at the docks. I am just here for a welfare check," Chris laughed and looked around.

"Well, thanks," Jonathan smiled.

"Is she still here?" Chris whispered.

Jonathan rolled his eyes at the smirk on Chris's face.

"Not for long," Renee's voice erupted behind them.

Jonathan turned to see the woman dressed, her sunglasses covering her face and her bag slung across her body like a shield.

"Good morning Miss Martin," Chris said. He was sensing the tension in the room.

"Chris, would you be so kind as to give me a ride back to the hotel?" She said cheerily.

"That won't be necessary," Jonathan said, walking toward the door to block her escape.

Renee pushed past him and out of the door—startling Chris, who had to step to the side to let her pass. Chris stared at Jonathan with his mouth gaping open like a hungry catfish.

Jonathan watched her open Chris's sedan door and slinked inside. He huffed angrily at Chris and lifted his hands up in the air in surrender.

He was stalking into the bedroom and slamming the door. He started gathering his laundry in the broken basket as he heard them pull out of the driveway.

10

Everything has busted over the last week. Dead batteries, oil changes, and stalled motors were resting all over the *Island Connections* building. Jonathan had been busy with Renee and neglecting some of his work duties. He thought it was worth stepping away to entertain the captivating woman, but now he wasn't so sure. The blazing heat or his anger was making his skin burn; he could not tell for sure.

The salt in the water reminded him of the salt in his wounds. The way Renee had been so quick to judge his lifestyle. It was not up to her standards, or he was not taking life severe enough for her. Either way, it irritated him, and losing himself in projects was his goal. His friend Chris did not intend to let that happen, and his persistence made him even more agitated.

"I'm not one to tell others how to handle their affairs," Chris started. "But you have been a mess all afternoon."

The ocean waves were attempting to drown out his voice. Jonathan knew there was truth to his observations. He remained silent, stewing in his feelings. Chris handed him a socket wrench and continued with his speech. His body leaned over the transom, watching Jonathan attach the motor to the outboard.

"She leaves tomorrow. Are you sure you want to leave it on a sour note?" Chris said.

Jonathan did not look up, cranking on the bolts more aggressively than necessary.

The sweat was beading on his forehead, and his polarized glasses blocked the sun's blinding reflection. Jonathan brought his hand up to wipe the sweat away. His frustration traveled to his limbs, and the sunglasses fell off his face, splashing into the water.

"Damnit," he grumbled, tossing the wrench into the boat and diving into the calm ocean. His hand searched the water but came up short.

When he resurfaced, with two strong strokes, he returned to the stern. Chris was waving a screwdriver.

"A big mess," he said, chuckling.

"Enough with the heckling," Jonathan snarled. "I am not in the mood."

"I'm just trying to help you, Boss," Chis shrugged. "As I said, I have never seen you act this way over a woman."

Jonathan stood on the ladder and squinted into the bright sunshine. "There is nothing I can do; she's going home, and I'm staying here."

"Yeah, but don't let her leave all angry. She is a nice lady," Chris said.

"She is stubborn," Jonathan corrected.

"So are you, my friend," Chris said. He smiled and leaned over the boat, grabbing the wrench and handing it to Jonathan.

"I've known you a long time; if there's one thing you're good at, it's fixing stuff," Chris said.

Jonathan yanked the tool from his hand and contemplated his words while he finished his task. He was right, but the trick with fixing motors is first finding out what's broken. With Renee's insecurities and divorce trauma, he didn't know if a few words would be enough.

"Easier said than done," Jonathan grumbled.

"Just trying to give you some words of wisdom, didn't say they would be worth listening to," Chris shrugged his shoulders and stood up to pace the dock. Their next tour was in a few minutes, and Jonathan decided to do it himself. He enjoyed the work, having been riding the same route since childhood and listening to his dad do it so many times. It would be good to be distracted from his feelings for a while.

Jonathan knew the advice his father would have would be worth taking. The man was a modern-day Solomon. He was constantly speaking words of wisdom. Jonathan didn't know it as a child, but now he would give anything to sit and hear his dad lecture him again.

What would you tell me, pops?

Jonathan shook the sadness off his bones and placed the tools in their metal box. He wiped his hands on his stained shirt and looked out into the horizon. The sunset tour will be a nice one; the humidity was low, as well as the wind. Both bred perfect conditions for the clouds to linger and the sky to light up with vibrant colors.

Chris was walking toward the boat as Jonathan jumped onto the dock. He moved past him into the office with a quick slap on his back. The two didn't always have to say it out loud; the gesture was enough of an apology as the words.

Jonathan went around the back and grabbed a clean shirt from his locker. Jonathan had a picture of his pops taped to the inside, and he stared at the man momentarily.

You would call me a fool for losing my temper. You would tell me to listen to Chris. That nothing in life worth having is easy, and you must fight like hell to keep it.

He shut the metal locker and stood back to think. Jonathan knew that it was out of his hands if the woman did not want to waste any more time with him. He sighed and realized the hold she had on his heart after such a short time. There was more to her than her stunning good looks. She was apprehensive about their age difference, but it was the last thing on his mind when he was around her. There was a mysterious allure that emanated from her smile. The way her eyes spoke volumes, and her body made him burn like a flare. She may be the only one to cut to that more profound level. Having known her for a few short days, Jonathan resolved it was better than never having met.

But do I love her? What is that saying? Better to have loved and lost than never to have loved at all?

He had never spoken those words to any woman. Worried it would be an omen or curse that would haunt him if he did. There had been no one in his life worth the expression. When he met Renee, it had been lust from the start; only now did he admit that the thought of her returning home was disturbing him. The fact that she was adamant about it ending when she left the island stung his pride.

Walking toward the office, he opened the door. The bell tied to the string above rang out, and he put on his best smile, anticipating a room full of waiting tourists. Instead, there was an empty space. He glanced down to check his watch.

The time is right; where is everyone?

Jonathan went behind the desk and looked for the key to the large touring boat. The hook was empty.

Chris must have it in his pocket.

He turned and went out the side door, wondering where Chris had lined up the spectators. As he stepped on the wooden dock, he heard the motor fire up, and the boat pulled away. Jonathan ran down the pier waving his arms. Chris stood, smiling at the helm. He lifted his hand and waved happily at Jonathan. He gave a thumbs up and turned to steer the ship away. Jonathan cursed him out in his mind. Angry that he was watching his distraction sail away.

He licked his lips at the thought and turned around. He wrung his hands together and wondered what he would do now that the evening was free. A few beers sounded like an equal distraction.

Leaning up against the wall was a woman in an oversized white sun hat. She wore large black glasses and was wearing a flowing teal dress. Her hair was as dark as night. She had a large beach bag resting by her feet. From where Jonathan stood, it was hard to see her. He approached, ready to apologize for her missing the departure time.

His head hung low out of instinct; he watched the dock boards pass under his feet as he got closer.

"I am sorry, Miss, but the tour-" Jonathan's voice trailed off when he looked up.

Renee stood up straight and adjusted her hat. She slid the glasses down the bridge of her nose and studied him with a dreamlike gaze.

"I sent Chris away with the tourists," she explained. "Would it be possible to book a private excursion?"

Her voice was sultry. The way her lips parted, and her chin raised at the last word had him twisted inside.

"I guess every man has his price," he answered.

"And how much would this cost me?" she said, tucking the hair behind her ear.

"We will negotiate at sea," he said.

11

Reluctantly Jonathan helped her aboard. Her visit had made him curious. He wondered what more she could say; she had thoroughly torn apart his lifestyle hours ago. Their earlier tiff had him riled and cranky. Her teal dress was doing a decent job of distracting him from his bad mood. She stepped carefully, and Jonathan remained by the rail, remembering their many unexpected dives into the surrounding waves. With her around, he had to anticipate a quick dip.

Jonathan reached inside his pocket and pulled out the key; with a sigh, he placed it in the ignition and gave it a crank.

The boat fired up and started toward the setting sun. The familiar vibration of the engine was soothing, and Jonathan relaxed his grip on the wheel. Steering them in and out of the channel markers and further out to sea. A few boats were making their way across the water, and Jonathan could spot Chris and the tour group sailing further ahead. For an instant, he wished he could switch places to avoid the uncomfortable quiet.

Jonathan stood, operating the ship and admiring the stunning scenery. Renee sat in stillness at the front. The hat was in her lap. Her dark hair flew carelessly behind her. With the magnificent glow of the sky surrounding her, she looked like a painting some Renaissance artist would have created hundreds of years ago.

She must have felt his eyes scanning her body; she turned her head slowly in his direction and allowed a smile to creep onto her face. He placed the engine to idle and walked up to the bow to join her.

Jonathan sat and remained silent. Relieved she had come back but guarded due to their last encounter. Jonathan could also be stubborn and was determined to let her do the talking. He leaned against the seat, spreading his arms on the top of the cushion like a gull and breathing in the air deeply.

Renee was watching him and moved to the edge of her seat. She leaned over, placing her hands on the exposed kneecaps under the vivid teal fabric. He pushed the impulses away while watching her rub her skin nervously.

"I owe you an apology," she said slowly.

He continued to stare at the gorgeous woman. His anger had faded, but the sting of her words was still fresh in his mind.

"I was out of line and, frankly, being a bitch," she said. "I am so used to saying whatever pops in my head, to always be on the defensive, I do not recognize when I am going too far."

Jonathan brought his arms down and crossed them over his chest. He chose his following words carefully as she waited.

"You are not wrong; I guess that's why it hit so hard," he said. "We aren't compatible outside of your vacation."

Renee looked out at the setting sun. A sadness had taken hold of her.

"I want to be," she whispered.

Jonathan leaned in. "Renee, I am lucky to have met you."

Renee smiled and closed her eyes.

"No, Jonathan, I am the lucky one. This week has been the most fun I have had in decades," she said. "I am always sabotaging myself from having a good time."

She opened her eyes, and Jonathan shrugged.

She is correct there.

"What you have taught me over the last few days is all about finding the balance," she said.

"Are we talking about life or on watercraft?" he chuckled.

Renee stuck her tongue out playfully. "I could not leave here without apologizing for my behavior."

"It's okay, really," Jonathan said. He shifted his weight in the seat.

"They say lawyers can be completely competent, but people feel we lack warmth," she sighed. "I am starting to see why we come off that way."

Jonathan snickered at the admission. He may have said something similar before.

"I used to be more carefree like you when I was in college," she said. "Then, everything changed when I had to pass the bar exam. I got so lost in my studies and then my career I forgot what it was like to have more than work."

"You love what you do, just like me," he said. "That's not a bad thing."

"I only do it for the money," she said, "It helps that I am good at it."

Jonathan nodded in understanding and softened his stare.

"I have been asking myself the last few days if I had wasted my life in the courtroom arguing," she said. "I have nothing to show for my work beside a ruthless reputation. My marriage was a lie, my only friends are colleagues, and I have muddled my first vacation with my mouth."

"You did not muddle anything," he said slowly, "you just need to work on your perspective."

She smiled. "You have helped me with that, thank you."

"My pleasure," he grinned. "It's never too late to change your voyage, set your course and sail for your dreams."

"Is that more of your father's advice?" she said.

"He was wise; what can I say?" he answered. "When you get home, take more time for yourself; that is my advice."

Renee leaned forward and unzipped the beach bag she had placed on the floor next to her feet. She pulled out two plastic cups, handing them to Jonathan.

"What is this?" Jonathan tried to look deeper inside the bag.

"I wanted to do something nice for our last night together," she said, "If I made it this far without you throwing me overboard."

"That thought is fleeting, don't worry," he laughed.

She pulled out a bottle of Champagne and removed the foil. The silver label shone against the glowing sunlight.

"Here, let me help you," Jonathan set the glasses down, and she passed them off willingly. His large hand engulfed the cork, twisting it quickly, and it popped into the air. Renee jumped at the sound and smiled.

"You are still so jumpy, huh?" he said, holding the cold bottle.

She grinned at him and returned to the bag. She was pulling out a small blanket and spreading it on the deck. There was a container of fruit, sandwiches, and cheese.

"You are like Mary Poppins with that bag," he chuckled, amazed at the spread. He was leaning over to take a slice of orange and pop it in his mouth. The citrus exploded, awakening his senses and clearing his mind.

She reached into the bag again and flashed the second bottle of Champagne.

"Just in case one didn't soften you up," she winked.

She set the glass bottle back inside and picked up the cups for Jonathan to pour. The tiny fizz of bubbles as the liquid hit the plastic made his mouth water. That and the sight of Renee's teeth biting at her perfectly full lips caused a ripple effect over his body.

"You brought me a picnic?" he said softly.

"I wanted to see what was so special about the sunset cruise," she said, "It has rave reviews."

He chuckled and brought the Champagne to his mouth, using the time to weigh his options.

One last night with this woman would only make it harder to watch her leave tomorrow, but if I don't taste her again, it will haunt me forever.

Renee did not allow him the choice. She pushed the cup aside and kissed him. Running her fingers through his long hair tugging it gently. When Renee's mouth parted, Jonathan's perturbations dissolved. The citrus that coated his mouth met the bubbles of the Champagne and only enhanced the flavor. The swipe of her tongue cleared his mind like a blank slate.

He scooped her up and laid her down on the thin blanket. Knocking the fruit and sandwiches over with his legs, he hovered over her body.

Renee's eyes burned into Jonathan with an unspoken desire. The overwhelming need made his body tense as she pushed his shoulder firmly and rolled him over on his back. She straddled him, her face illuminated by the light falling over the horizon. Her arms reached up and pushed her mane behind her in the sudden gust of wind. She lifted the bottom of her dress, pulling it slowly over her shoulders and tossing it to the floor behind her. She was completely exposed. She looked like a Goddess floating above him with her tan skin and wild hair. Jonathan felt himself sinking into the blanket, absorbing the sight.

"Renee, you are so beautiful," he whispered, grabbing her hips with his painted arms.

A strong and determined woman pinned him down. She circled her hips in a compelling rhythm. He wanted to tear himself from his restricting clothes and join her in the enticing freedom. Jonathan decided to wait and let the captivating dance play out.

The clouds were on fire with pinks and oranges as the last sliver of light sank into the ocean. As Renee leaned in, Jonathan closed his eyes.

This is how the heavens kiss the earth.

12

───────

The day was cloudy and enhanced the finish line of infatuation with an unspoken gloom. The gray sky was appropriate for the events ahead, only adding to the chill in the air. After a beautiful night of passion and star gazing, when Jonathan returned to the boat and escorted Renee to her hotel room, he wished he could control time and make the previous night last forever.

He had borrowed Chris's car, wanting to drive Renee to the ferry. He could not send her off in a dingy cab. He waited as she gathered her belongings, already packed and waiting by the door. She smiled sadly at the room as he rushed to pick up her luggage.

"That's it; I think I grabbed everything," she said.

She opened the door for him, and he stepped through. The elevator seemed to shrink around them as the reality of her departure set into Jonathan's stomach. He had already suggested she stay, which ruffled her feathers, so he kept his aching—knowing that his suggestions would be futile.

As she checked out, he packed her suitcase in the trunk. She joined him a minute later, and Jonathan started the car.

"One last tour?" she smiled.

He grinned back, but his expression was deceiving his feelings. "Yes, Ma'am."

They traveled down the strip. Renee tried to make small talk, but Jonathan was distracted. She pulled out her cell and scrolled through the pictures she had taken over the last few days. She was commenting on their adventures and the beauty of the island. Renee rested her hand on his thigh. Her tender gesture meant more to him than she knew.

They reached the ferry slip and exited the car. Jonathan retrieved her bag and walked her toward the ramp. She turned, and he swooped her up in his arms.

"I wish there were something I could stay to keep you here," he whispered. His face was inches from Renee's lips.

"Jonathan, I-," she stuttered.

"I know, but I need to make it clear to you," he said, desperation consuming his voice. "I know we have just met; I know how crazy it sounds."

Renee closed her eyes as if trying to shut out his words. His grip on her body only tightened as she braced for impact.

"There is a chance this is more than just passion; there is a chance this could be real," he said.

She winced. Jonathan could tell he had struck a nerve but didn't care.

"Renee-" he started, but she interrupted the words. Her eyes opened wide, and she did the only thing she could break his concentration. She placed her lips quickly on his mouth. Jonathan was helpless with her rebuttal.

She backed away after a long embrace. Jonathan searched her face for a hint of persuasion.

"I had a wonderful week," she said. Her eyes were tearing, but her voice remained steady. "You will find happiness, Jonathan. I am sure of it."

"What about your happiness Renee?" he said sadly.

"It may be too late for me," she whispered. "I am glad I took this trip. I am happy I met you."

"It's never too late," he said, releasing her.

She frowned and continued to back away toward her waiting escape. "Goodbye, Jonathan."

Renee turned and boarded the ferry. Jonathan stood at the metal fence and watched as the ship moved slowly away from the slip. His heart felt like it could shatter as he let the woman go.

The fog horn blew, adding insult to injury. The sound mocked his emotions and rattled his core. He remained on the fence until the boat disappeared, knowing he had let something great slip away.

The ride back to the office was so lonely he could choke. Jonathan walked into the building, and the ringing bell startled his thoughts. Tossing the keys to Chris, he made his way out to the boats. He grabbed his tools and a beer from the mini-fridge.

The vacation is over. It is time to get back to work.

The following two weeks dragged on. Time had seemed to move at a snail's pace while Jonathan consumed himself with work. It was difficult not to think of the woman; every time the waves crashed, the breeze blew or the sun set. Everything around him made Jonathan reflect on her enchanting smile. He was starting to believe he could never escape his hollow feeling.

Chris did his best to cheer up his friend. They had gone out for drinks frequently after work. However, Jonathan was not the best company. The dark clouds from the ferry had attached themselves to the man, and they hung onto him like a barnacle on the bottom of a ship. His attitude was sharp, and he often took out his frustrations on anyone in his path.

After the first few days had passed and there was no call, he began to accept his feelings were not reciprocated, and he needed to press on. Before Renee left, he had given his cell number. Hopeful that when she returned, she would reach out and confess the mistake she had made.

The business had been steady, and it kept him occupied. Chris had given him a list of projects that needed tending to, and he assaulted the tasks gratefully.

Jonathan called Chris and told him to cover the office. It was early morning, and the conditions were prime for fishing. Jonathan needed a break and attempted to reset. Chris happily complied, hoping Jonathan could catch a better outlook along with some fish.

He cast a line in the water and sat back, reflecting on the woman and casting his hopes away into the deep blue water.

It is time to let her go. You have held out, hoping for a change of heart. There is no use dwelling on it.

His pole bowed as the line tightened. Something pulled hard under him. His heart jumped into his throat as he sat up excitedly. He was reeling the rod hard, using his strength to drag the fish to the surface. As he struggled against the mysterious catch, the ship's radio blasted out behind him.

Chris's voice came through the static. "Hey Boss, we have a situation."

Jonathan groaned in annoyance, pulling the catch out of the water.

Not now, Chris.

"We have another ski dead in the water," Chirs barked over the radio.

Jonathan's mind returned to his last rescue mission, and he raised his arms quickly, pulling the pole over his shoulder. The clear line snapped, and he stumbled backward into the boat.

Damnit.

He threw the pole to the floor and marched to the receiver. He was asking Chris for the direction of the craft. The passenger had called complaining the jet ski would not start. Chris explained the projected coordinates based on the description of the shore.

Jonathan started the ship towards the floating tourist. He was lecturing himself to avoid repeating the same mistakes of the weeks before. He racked his brain about the battery. He was frustrated with the brand and the inability to hold a charge. When he returned, he would be sure to order from a different vendor.

He eventually spotted the floating craft. His scowl was stuck on his face. Forcing himself to grin, he awaited the customer's complaints, knowing they were again justified. The familiar scene of a damsel in distress was coming into view, and his heart felt the familiar stab. He shut off the engine and let his ship drift closer.

Just once, could it be a guy? What is up with the universe teasing me with women?

She was leaning over the front of the ski, searching in the compartment.

"Hey there, can I help?" he called out kindly.

His eyes went wide as the woman stood up and turned around.

"What kind of business are you running here?" Renee smiled at him.

Jonathan's body was electric. The shock of her voice hit his ears like a taser. Before he knew it, he was leaping off the ship's side and diving deep. When he resurfaced, he found Renee waiting in the water, bobbing up and down in her life preserver. He grabbed the vest and dragged it closer, her body weightless and floating freely.

"You came back," he said between the salty kisses on her lips.

Her eyes searched his face in the bright sunshine. "I never should have left."

Jonathan kissed her again as the tide pushed them closer together. He smiled at his most incredible catch, knowing he wouldn't let this one get away.

EPILOGUE

enee lay sprawled out on Jonathan's sheets, watching the waves crash into the shore. Everything about the view reflected the tranquility and peace she felt inside. The voice inside her head had stopped its constant doubt the minute Renee made it home and shocked her office with her sudden decision. It had only taken a few steps into the cold office building for her to realize she wanted to trade in her pantsuit for a summer dress. Her mind had been on Jonathan since boarding the ferry. His unspoken words were looming inside.

She continued to deny the possibility of a life outside her work. Renee was reminded of her unhappiness when she returned. Jonathan had brought so much more than a good time in bed; he had shown her that life did not always need to be black and white. There were colors in the world she had been ignoring, and she wanted to waste no time splattering them across her dull canvas.

When she announced she was leaving the firm, her colleagues gasped dramatically. She beamed at their reactions, knowing this was her first act of recklessness. Over the next few days, she had arranged to sell her large house, pack up most of her things for donation, and choose a few items to take. Most of her belongings felt like a filler for the void. Renee reassured herself of the decision by looking at her two suitcases and noting how they were all she owned that had any importance. She made the necessary travel arrangements and spent the last days tying loose ends.

I had spent my life in Austin but needed the house and designer furniture to show for it. I can easily leave this all here; it means nothing.

She remembered how boarding the ferry had her nerves fluttering. Not sure if Jonathan could forgive her for her abandonment. Her leaving it all behind was romantic, but was it enough?

She gazed out the window and sighed. Jonathan was not what she expected to find on her trip to discover herself. He had a way of opening doors for her she never knew existed. She felt like she was racing through life with her head down, too focused and unable to afford distraction. If she had learned anything from him since returning, the biggest regret she could have was not slowing down and savoring time.

It was never too late to change.

Her thoughts were interrupted by Jonathan kicking in the door lightly with his foot. His hands were complete with a wooden tray.

"I thought you had left for work," she said, surprised.

"I took the day off," he smiled and walked closer. He was shirtless, and she appreciated the sight.

"Good," she smiled and kneeled forward on the mattress.

"Calm down, vixen," he laughed. "There is plenty of time for that."

She sank back against the headboard and pouted playfully. "What do you have there?"

The delicious smell filled her nostrils as Jonathan lowered the tray and presented her breakfast proudly. There was a fried egg nestled around slices of toast. She looked up and met his grin.

"You were paying attention," she said, acknowledging the perfectly prepared egg.

"Well," he started, setting the tray before her, "it was my third attempt."

Renee let the thought of cracked eggs and burnt pans slip from her thoughts. Jonathan must have read her mind and laughed.

"I cleaned up and ate the eggshells," he said quickly.

She let out a sigh of relief. "I am trying."

"I know, and so am I," he laughed.

She broke into the yolk and watched the yellow silk spread onto the plate.

Jonathan pulled out a small box. The familiar velvet case sent a chill over her skin. The tiny voice of doubt returned long enough to spread an edgy look across her face.

Renee reached out with trembling hands, prepared to push it away.

"Open it," he said, his tone serious.

She looked at him with warning and took the box, prying it apart. Inside sat a silver wreath surrounding a beautiful golden pearl. Renee masked her sigh of relief and looked at the necklace with admiration.

"King Neptune," he pointed to his tattooed arm, "was enthralled with the beautiful nymph Salacia."

He pointed next to his other arm. The portrait of the beautiful woman with a crown of seaweed was staring at her with a familiar powerful expression. The ink on his skin twitched from his movements, bringing the picture to life. She was perched in a chariot of pearls, pulled by an army of seahorses.

"She represented the Goddess of salt water and keeper of the sea. King Neptune wanted to marry Salacia, but she ran from him and hid in the ocean. Neptune eventually persuaded her to return and share his throne," Jonathan explained.

"I don't want to marry again," she said, running her finger over the golden pearl.

Jonathan grabbed the box from her hand, removed the chain, and walked to the side of the bed, clasping the pearl around her delicate neck.

He returned to sit beside her on the mattress.

"I know that, and I wouldn't expect you to," he said carefully. "Though I want to invite you to share my throne."

He waited patiently for her response. "Of course, but I am not wearing a seaweed crown."

Jonathan chuckled, relief washing over his body. He placed the box down on the tray.

"What are we doing today, Captain?" she asked, taking a bite of eggs. She moaned in approval.

"I was thinking, after breakfast, we could walk the shore," he said, looking outside.

"I have a better idea," she whispered, pushing the tray away.

She leaned in and wrapped her arms around his neck.

"I want to hear all about it," Jonathan moaned against her forearm.

Renee pushed him backward and laughed. "My life has been full of words and arguments. How about I show you instead?"

Jonathan's eyes softened. "Proceed, Miss Martin."

She bit his neck at his poorly-timed courtroom joke and giggled on his flesh.

For the first time in her life, Renee was happy. She dove deep into Jonathan's firm grasp, pausing only to come up for air. They spent hours floating in and out of each other's arms.

"I could drown in this moment," he whispered.

His words sent her over the edge, like a wave crashing into a shore of ecstasy. She felt like the queen of saltwater taming her wild King.